W9-BTL-207

THE GREAT SCHOOL LUNCH REBELLION
HAS BEGUN!

DUCK!

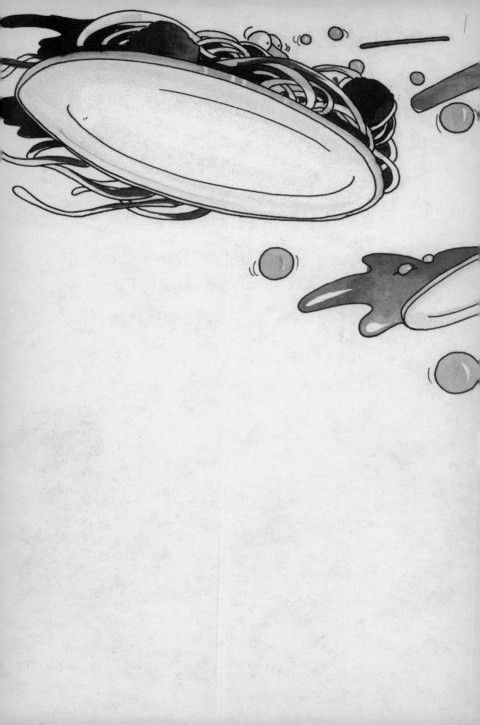

The Great School Lunch Rebellion

By David Greenberg

Illustrated by Maxie Chambliss

A BANTAM SKYLARK BOOK®
NEW YORK · TORONTO · LONDON · SYDNEY · AUCKLAND

RL 1, 005-008

THE GREAT SCHOOL LUNCH REBELLION
A Bantam Skylark Book / March 1989

Skylark Books is a registered trademark of Bantam Books,
a division of Bantam Doubleday Dell Publishing Group, Inc.
Registered in U.S. Patent and Trademark Office and elsewhere.

All rights reserved.
Copyright © 1989 by David Greenberg.
Text illustrations and cover art copyright © 1989 by Maxie Chambliss.
No part of this book may be reproduced or transmitted in any form or by any means,
electronic or mechanical, including photocopying, recording, or by any information
storage and retrieval system, without permission in writing from the publisher.
For information address: Bantam Books.

*If you purchased this book without a cover you should be aware that this book is stolen
property. It was reported as "unsold and destroyed" to the publisher and neither the
author nor the publisher has received any payment for this "stripped book."*

ISBN 0-553-15551-2

Published simultaneously in the United States and Canada

Bantam Books are published by Bantam Books, a division of Bantam Doubleday Dell
Publishing Group, Inc. Its trademark, consisting of the words "Bantam Books" and the
portrayal of a rooster, is Registered in U.S. Patent and Trademark Office and in other
countries. Marca Registrada, Bantam Books, 666 Fifth Avenue, New York, New York 10103

PRINTED IN THE UNITED STATES OF AMERICA

CW   14 13 12 11 10 9 8 7 6 5 4

With all my love to Sharon, Justin,
Ryan, and Snout (Chairman Emeritus,
Belly Rubs International) D.G.

For those wonderful Bald Head O'Keefes M.C.

The Great School Lunch Rebellion

Oh, they're great to poison squirrels
But I wouldn't recommend them
For healthy boys 'n' girls

I

Do they ever serve you lunches at your school
That to tell the truth are positively sick?
No one knows for sure what they are made of
But throw them at the ceiling and they stick

Do they ever serve you lunches at your school
That are really almost frightening to eat?
You have to stab them quickly with your knife
Or they'll hop away on grimy little feet

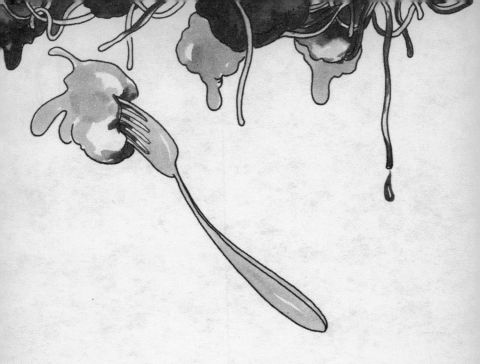

Do they ever serve you lunches
So terribly disgusting
When you touch them with your fork
It actually starts rusting?

If you've ever eaten lunches such as these
Then I'm certain you'll be able to relate
To the story of our Great School Lunch Rebellion
And our truly unexpected fate.

II

The soup they serve us at our school
Must be made from monkey spit
Chunks of chewed-up bubble gum
And sweaty catcher's mitt

None of us can stand it
Except my buddy Jay
But Jay eats almost anything
Once, he ate a tray

The tater tots have bones in them
We think they're human toes
Matt and Kim found eyeballs
In Monday's sloppy Joes

There's a meat sauce on the pizza
That could kill a polar bear
Though Justin says he likes it
For conditioning his hair

And if you think I'm lying
I'd like to see you try it
How come teachers bring their lunch?
You'll never see *them* buy it.

Why only Jay (who ate the tray)
Eats here without qualms
Says Jay, "I really love the meals
They're twice as good as Mom's"

So you really can't blame Ezra
'Cuz he hid his franks 'n' beans
In his pencil case and sneakers
And the pockets of his jeans

And it's logical that Phyllis
Gave her chicken lunch to Linda
Though Linda sure surprised us
When she chucked it out the winda

And that's when our rebellion
Actually began
I really wish you'd been there
It was positively grand!

For loony Linda's chicken
Clobbered Suzy Dole
Who hurled back a hamburger
Which zonkered Billy Cole

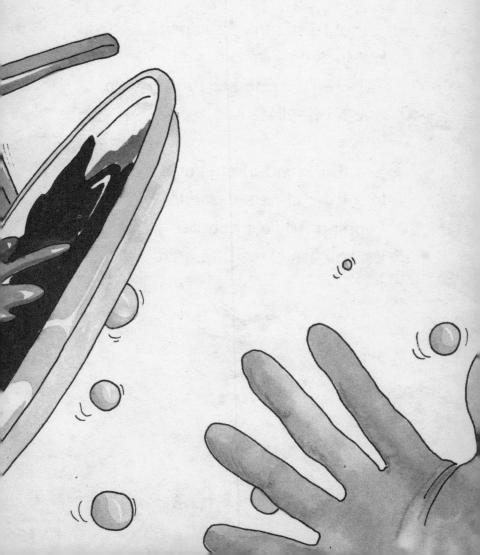

"Stop!" cried Miss O'Martin
"I'll only count to ten"
But no one seemed to hear her
Though she screamed out once again

"Stop! I'll get the principal!"
But luck was on our side
For as she turned to run for help
She took a little ride ...

See, Billy kind of staggered
Into Ed McKee's dessert
Flipping Eddie's noodles
Down Miss O'Martin's shirt

Miss O'Martin squealed
Slipped on a banana
Lost her wig in Sarah's soup
And fell in the piana

Then our principal ran in
Skidded on a carton
Cartwheeled through some meatballs
And crashed on Miss O'Martin

Wow, splat in the piano!
And everyone fell quiet
Till rowdy Ryan locked them in
And kids began to riot!

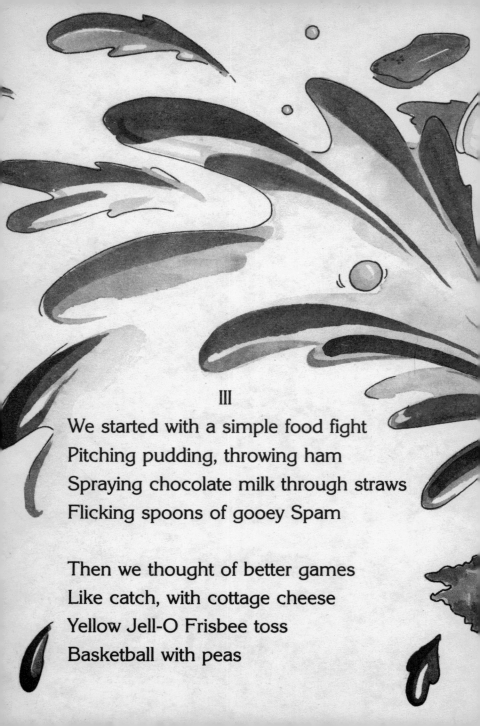

III

We started with a simple food fight
Pitching pudding, throwing ham
Spraying chocolate milk through straws
Flicking spoons of gooey Spam

Then we thought of better games
Like catch, with cottage cheese
Yellow Jell-O Frisbee toss
Basketball with peas

Sharon's face got zapped
With a piece of wet baloney
Janette was buried to her neck
In tons of macaroni

Joe shampooed Sarah's hair
With chunky peanut butter
Mark and Ken were taking turns
Egging one another

The floor was inches deep in soup
Mountained high with moldy cheese
Kids were sliding down the mountains
Using lunchroom trays for skis

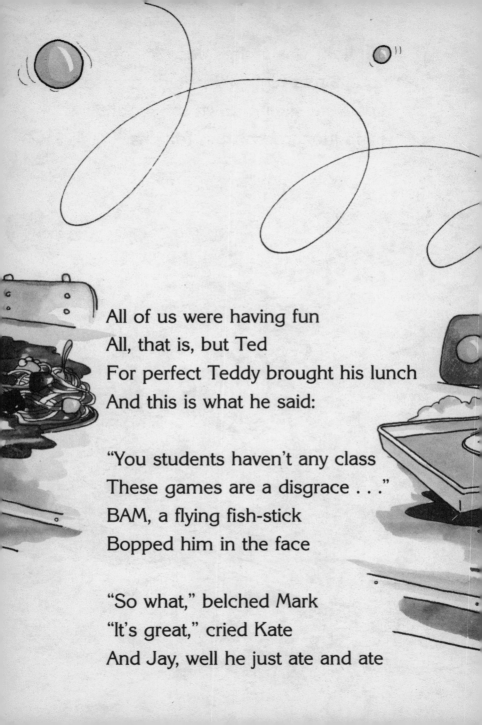

All of us were having fun
All, that is, but Ted
For perfect Teddy brought his lunch
And this is what he said:

"You students haven't any class
These games are a disgrace . . ."
BAM, a flying fish-stick
Bopped him in the face

"So what," belched Mark
"It's great," cried Kate
And Jay, well he just ate and ate

"You're really gonna get it"
Threatened fishy Ted
"When teachers see what's going on
You're positively dead"

"No way," said Jay
"It's all okay
At recess time we'll sneak away"

"Yeah," said Joe
"They'll never know
Teachers here are really slow"

Said Ted, "You've got it coming
You'll surely get suspended
When teachers find out what you've done
Your days at school are ended"

And with those words, like instant magic
Something happened strange and neat
(Though hardly could we know
That it signaled our defeat)

"Wow," laughed Jane
"It sounds insane
But I just felt a drop of rain"

"Me too," yelled Dawn
"Right on," cheered John
"Someone switched the sprinklers on!"

IV

And guess who switched the sprinklers on?
Come on, take a guess
Yup, Jay's the one who did it
What a splendid mess!

Water quickly started rising
Past the chairs and tabletops
Kids were splashing, swimming, sinking
Bobbing by in bowls and pots

And remember the piano?
It was floating in the lake
With the principal and Miss O'Martin
Banging to escape

And yet the water still was rising
Things were looking scary now
"Let's get out of here," cried Debby
Gurgled Jack, "But how?"

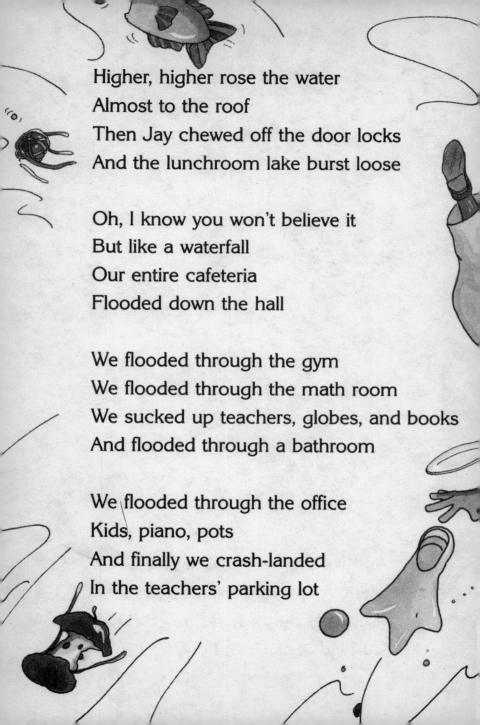

Higher, higher rose the water
Almost to the roof
Then Jay chewed off the door locks
And the lunchroom lake burst loose

Oh, I know you won't believe it
But like a waterfall
Our entire cafeteria
Flooded down the hall

We flooded through the gym
We flooded through the math room
We sucked up teachers, globes, and books
And flooded through a bathroom

We flooded through the office
Kids, piano, pots
And finally we crash-landed
In the teachers' parking lot

And there was the piano
With the grown-ups both inside
It had landed sideways upside down
"Let us out!" they cried

But none of us could open it
'Cuz no one had the key
Till perfect Teddy found it
And swiftly set them free

"We're saved," sighed Miss O'Martin
With teardrops in her eyes
"Teddy," said the principal
"You deserve a prize"

"And as for all you others,"
Said the principal with sorrow
"You'll regret your misbehavior
When I punish you tomorrow."

V

Next morning after flag salute
We hadn't long to wait
Till the principal announced to us
Our terrifying fate

"You were juvenile delinquents!
You were disrespectful, crude!
You kids," he said, "do not deserve
Delicious gourmet food"

"Therefore I suspend you brats
(All but Teddy here)
From dining in our lunchroom
The remainder of the year"

"However," spoke the principal
"We have a treat in store
For that special one among you
Who was well behaved, mature"

"It's our pleasure, Ted, to give you
An extraordinary treat:
Free school-lunches all year long
All that you can eat!"

"Today's school lunch in fact
Was created just for you
As a mark of our deep gratitude
It's camel liver stew!"

Teddy seemed to lose his balance
Somebody groaned, "yuck"
"Oh," sighed Jay, "it isn't fair
Ted has all the luck."

VI

So the Great School Lunch Rebellion
Is now over with and done
To be absolutely honest
It was loads and loads of fun

Yes it's true that we were punished
'Cuz our principal got mad
But a punishment, we found out,
Isn't always bad.

About the Author

DAVID GREENBERG is the author of *Slugs* (Atlantic-Little Brown) and *Teaching Poetry to Children* (Portland State University). He travels to schools and conferences around the country, speaking about writing and education, reading his poetry, and participating in writing workshops and education forums. Raised in New York, he currently lives in Portland, Oregon, with his wife Sharon, his sons Justin and Ryan, a Houndus Horriblus named Snout, a Fiendish Feline named Snowy, and other carnivores too numerous to mention.

About the Illustrator

MAXIE CHAMBLISS grew up in New Jersey and studied art at the Rhode Island School of Design. She has illustrated more than twenty children's books, including *Find That Puppy!* and *Chase That Pig!* in Bantam Little Rooster's Show Me! series. Her studio is located in Somerville, Massachusetts, where she lives with her husband Davis and their two children, Sarah and Morgan, and monster dog Bill.